Tell Me *More*

the importance of avoiding jealousy and anger

Thirtysix.org

In memory of my father-in-law
Chaim Avraham Eliyahu *ben* Moshe Yosef, ז"ל
who told a good story, and,

my mother-in-law
Raizel Charnah *bas* Moshe Eliezer, ז"ל
who loved the stories I told.

I would like to express tremendous gratitude to *Hashem Yisborach* for allowing me to work on this second book for children. I pray that it will only inspire love of God and of His Torah.

I also thank **Gavriel** and **Chana Sneider** for helping make this book a reality.

Thank you very much to **R. Horovitz** for the amazing illustrations that grace these pages. She can be reached at 053-413-6753.

BS"D

Tell Me More

The Importance of Avoiding Jealousy and Anger

ISBN 9798366448420

Questions can be sent to: pinchasw@thirtysix.org.

Published by:
Thirtysix.org
22 Yitzchak Road
Telzstone, Kiryat Yearim
Israel 9083800

The positive feedback from the first book, *Boruch Hashem*, inspired me to turn this into a series of Shmuli Levenstein books to teach some of the most important lessons of life. The topics of jealousy and anger are obviously important because of their very destructive role in history, including Torah history. Jealousy even played a central role in the building of the Jewish nation during the births of the *Shevatim* (12 Tribes), and the sale of Yosef.

Both jealousy and anger are "natural" reactions to many situations, especially as affluence and competition increase in daily life. It is crucial to teach children as early as possible the importance of avoiding such negative emotions so that they can grow up to be loving and respectful adults. *Shalom bayis* (peace in the home) on all levels depend upon it, especially within a person.

Once-upon-a-time,
A very long time ago,
Hashem made the world,
And gave mankind a go.

So He put him in a garden,
So beautiful and complete,
But mankind gave it up,
For something forbidden to eat.

It was knowledge he wanted,
So he ate forbidden fruit,
And he learned the hard way,
Of a whole different route.

When we use our minds well,
And ask a good question,
We correct our mistake,
And earn Hashem's affection.

As the *rebi* waited for someone to answer his question, he noticed Shmuli was daydreaming again. But he did not feel the need to call across the room and snap him out of his thoughts, like he might have six months ago. He learned that when Shmuli daydreamed, it was usually about something good and resulted in a good question.

"Maybe you want to ask *me* a question?" the *rebi* said, trying to get some kind of response from his students.

He got one. It was Shmuli.

The *rebi* smiled. "Yes, Shmuli," he said.

Shmuli thought for a second more, and then asked his question. "How could Kayin kill his brother Hevel?"

None of the other students were impressed by the question, so they just continued to daydream on their own.

"What do you mean, Shmuli?" the *rebi* asked.

"Well," he said, considering his words, "my brothers and I fight at home sometimes. . .and. . .and sometimes one of us might. . .ah. . .well. . .hit the other. . ."

There were some giggles around the room, which distracted Shmuli for a moment, but then he continued.

". . .but we'd never be able to really hurt each other. . . and. . .*Chas v'Challilah*. . ."

Shmuli couldn't even say the words.

The *rebi*, once again, was impressed by Shmuli's sensitivity and thoughtfulness. And to impress the others as well, he said, "That's a great question that I have asked myself for years. . ."

As planned, all of the other little heads around the room perked up and turned towards the *rebi*, as if they just missed

something important.

"In fact," the *rebi* continued, "I know a lot of psychologists who have asked the same question."

"Psy. . .psychol. . ." Shmuli tried. Too many syllables.

"Psychologists," the *rebi* repeated. "Those are people who we pay to help us understand ourselves better, so that we can be better people."

Shmuli thought for a moment. At first he looked confused, but then he looked excited and said, "Then that makes *Hashem* a psy. . .pschol. . ."

The *rebi* smiled. Shmuli never ceased to amaze him. He wasn't necessarily the *smartest* in the class, but he had this way of seeing things. . .

"Yes," the *rebi* said still smiling, "I guess it would."

When the *rebi* saw that the rest of the *talmidim* were beginning to drift away into their own worlds, he decided to

Parashat `Bereshit´
"kol dmey
elay min

bring them back by asking the question to them.

"Shmuli's question is an important one for all of us," he said, trying to catch the eyes of as many *talmidim* as he could. "How would you answer it? How does a person even get to a point where they can hurt someone so badly? I feel bad if I just drive into a butterfly!"

The *talmidim* liked that, which drew them back in.

A hand went up at the back of the class.

"You have an answer, Dovid?" the *rebi* asked.

Dovid enthusiastically shook his head up-and-down.

"Share it with us please," the *rebi* encouraged.

Dovid thought for a moment, and then he said, "Once when I was driving with my *abba* someone almost hit our car. My *abba* got very angry because it was so dangerous. . . I never saw my *abba* angry like that before."

Everyone was paying attention now. All of a sudden, each

one had their own similar story. The *rebi* had a look of concern on his face. He didn't know what would come out of Dovid's story, and he felt like he was hearing personal information that might be embarrassing to Dovid and his *abba*. It might be *loshon hara*. As he considered what to do, Dovid continued.

"After, my *abba* said to me. 'Do you see how angry I just got?' I nodded yes."

Dovid nodded his head to show what he meant.

"'I want you to learn something today from me, okay?' my *abba* said. I nodded yes again."

Again he nodded, which made some of the boys giggle. They got the idea already.

"'Do you see how angry I just got?' my *abba* asked. ' Well, I want you to know that it was not the right thing to do. What the other driver did was very dangerous, but getting angry was not the right way to respond. That was just my *yetzer hara* using the situation to make me angry. It knows when we're weak, and

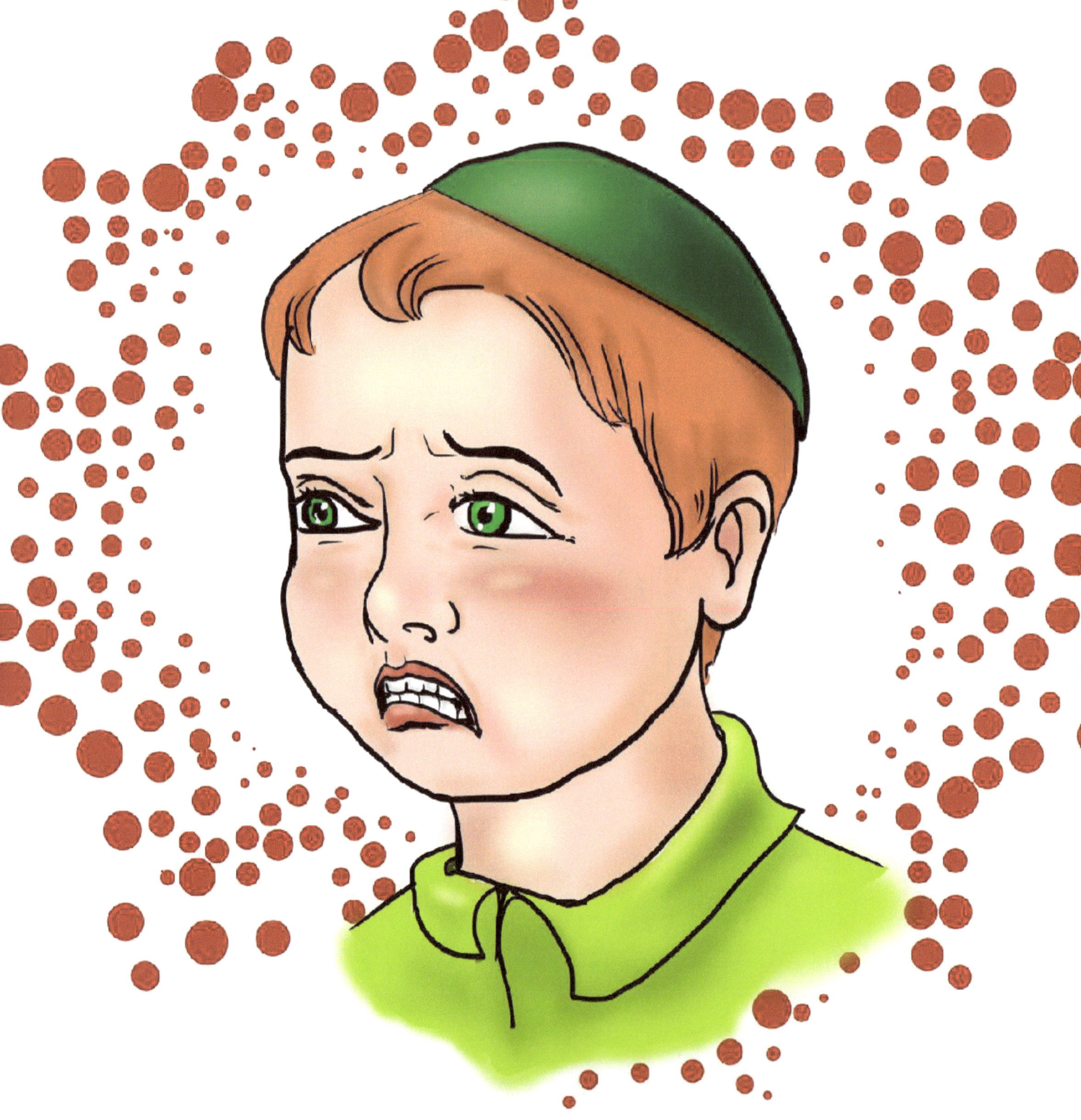

takes advantage of the situation to get us to do a *chet*.'"

The *rebi* was impressed. He was impressed by what Dovid's father had said to his son at such a moment, and impressed that Dovid still remembered it so well. "Very good," he told Dovid, and then added to it. "It's a very good point to remember," he said. "We all get angry sometimes because we feel that someone has done something wrong to us. Sometimes we even blame *Hashem* for the wrong, and get angry at Him, *Chas v'Shalom*."

Yitzi put up his hand now. The *rebi* turned to him and said, "What would you like to say, Yitzi."

"Well. . .um. . .my neighbor is angry at *Hashem*. I heard him tell my *abba* one day. He lost something. . .and now he's angry at *Hashem*."

The *rebi* was speechless for a moment. He had no idea that the class would go this way, or that his students would have so much to talk about on the topic. With the exception of one or

two, all of the *talmidim* seemed interested in the discussion. It was amazing what they thought about at such a young age, and how they dealt with it. He loved teaching his students, but he was learning something new from them this time.

Before the *rebi* knew it, there was only five minutes left to go before the break. He wanted to wrap things up so they could focus on something new once recess was over.

"What I am hearing from all of you," he said, "is that anger is something that the *yetzer hara* tries to make us feel, so that we will do things we don't really want to do."

Some of the boys unconsciously nodded in agreement.

"Sometimes people can become so angry that they can do something bad that they will later wish they hadn't, right?"

Again the boys nodded in agreement.

"The *Rambam* says that every *middah* has a good and bad side. This means that sometimes it is good to feel a certain way, and sometimes it is not. For example, it is wrong to be jealous

about what someone else has. But it is good to be jealous of someone else's learning accomplishments. . .if it makes you want to try harder and do the same. *Chazal* call that *kinas sofrim.*"

He gave the boys a moment to absorb that.

"The only *middah*," the *rebi* continued, "that the *Rambam* says should not be used at all, even for something good, is *ka'as* (anger). It's too dangerous. . .because a person will think they're getting angry for a good reason but it ends up being a bad reason. So the *Rambam* says, it is better to stay away from anger altogether."

Then, as if reading their minds, the *rebi* added, "Let's ALL try to remember that. . .me included."

As the boys smiled the recess bell went off. They all jumped into action and began to move in each direction. As the classroom cleared out, the *rebi* noticed that one boy was still sitting down. It was Shmuli, and he was writing something in his

"שבע שבתות תמימות תהינה.

notebook.

"Aren't you going to run out like the rest of the boys?" he asked.

Shmuli looked up at the *rebi* and said, "Just a moment. I just want to write down what we talked about. I don't want to get angry ever again, so I want to remember what we spoke about."

"That's very good, Shmuli."

Then Shmuli held up his notebook for his rebi to see, and showed him what looked like two faces on the same page. One looked angry, and the other was smiling. But there was a big X through the angry one. The *rebi* smiled.

"This should help," he told his *rebi*. "From now on, any time I get angry, I'm going to take out this picture and look at it."

"Wonderful," he told Shmuli. Then looking more closely at the picture, he asked Shmuli, "What's that squiggly line on top

חומש
בראשית

of the head with the X through it."

"A snake," Shmuli answered. "That's to remind me that it's not me who wants to get angry, but my *yetzer hara*."

The *rebi* found himself chuckling. "That's great," he said, and gave him a blessing. "*Hashem* should bless you to always be so smart, and He should always help you to never get angry."

Shmuli smiled, and answered, "Amen!"

Then he put his notebook and pen down on his desk and made for the door like the rest of the boys had done. Just before going out, Shmuli stopped as if he forgot something. Turning towards his *rebi*, who had already returned to his desk, he said, "Thank you *rebi*," causing his *rebi* to smile. Within a moment Shmuli was outside with the rest of the boys, while his *rebi* inside still enjoyed the moment of appreciation.

פרשת בראשית
״קול דמי
צועקים אלי מן האדמה״

Abba: father

Kayin: Cain

Hevel: Abel

Talmidim: students

Loshon hara: evil tongue (derogatory speech about another person)

Yetzer hara: evil inclination

Hashem: The Name (God)

Chas v'Chalilah/Chas v'Shalom: God forbid

Middah: measure (character trait)

Chazal: and acronym for "our rabbis, may they be remembered for blessing"

Kinas sofrim: jealousy of scribes (jealous of another's Torah learning)

Rambam: acronym for Rabbi Moshe ben Maimon

Rabbi Pinchas Winston has written over 100 books to date on various different Torah topics, most of which are available through Amazon, or the Thirtysix.org online bookstore.

Write to **pinchasw@thirtysix.org** for additional information.

thirtysix.org

www.ingramcontent.com/pod-product-compliance
Lightning Source LLC
Chambersburg PA
CBHW042127110726
48006CB00003B/788
9798366448420